STEGOSAURUS

Especially for Jack Anthony, with love

First published in Great Britain in 1996
by Macdonald Young Books Ltd
Campus 400
Maylands Avenue
Hemel Hempstead
Herts HP2 7EZ

Text © 1996 M. Christina Butler
Illustrations © 1996 Val Biro

Typeset in 20pt Plantin by
Goodfellow & Egan Ltd, Cambridge
Printed and bound in Belgium by
Proost International Book Productions

British Library Cataloguing in Publication Data available

ISBN 0 7500 1833 X
ISBN 0 7500 1834 8

DIPLODOCUS

TRICERATOPS

ARCHIE

ARCHIE
THE UGLY DINOSAUR

M. Christina Butler

Illustrated by
VAL BIRO

MACDONALD YOUNG BOOKS

Not all dinosaurs were big.
Archie was very small . . .

Much smaller than his friends.

Wherever they went,
Archie's legs were so small,

he was always left behind.

And whatever they did,

Archie was usually in the way.

He tried everything,

but nothing seemed to make him bigger.

Then Archie woke up one morning and
FELT he was growing at last.
But when he looked down at himself,
he was covered all over in little spikes!

Everyone laughed when they saw him.

They laughed so much,

that Archie ran away, deep into the forest.

When Archie had gone,
the big dinosaurs
began blaming
each other.
"You shouldn't have
laughed at him,"
said Triceratops.

"Well you laughed first,"
cried Stegosaurus.
Diplodocus was
thoughtful.
"The forest is
a dangerous place
for a small dinosaur,"
she said.
"We'd better find
him before the
big Rexes do."

They began to look at once.

They searched by day,

and they searched . . .

by night.

They came to the
mountains where the
big Rexes lived.
"I don't like it here,"
Triceratops whispered.

So they stopped and called out,

"ARCHIE ... ARE YOU THERE?"

Suddenly the big Rexes
came out with a
ROAR!

"Run!" cried Diplodocus.
"Archie isn't here!"

"Yes I am!" answered a voice.

"I'm up here!"

Archie had grown into a BIRD!
A beautiful ARCHAEOPTERYX.

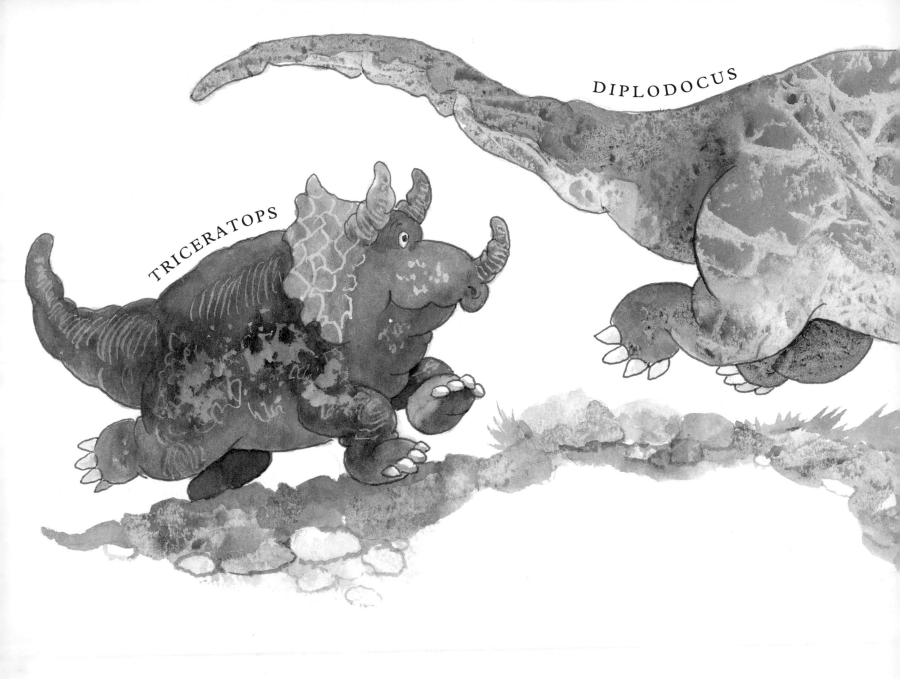

ARCHAEOPTERYX

STEGOSAURUS